Cat Jumped In!

by Tess Weaver

Illustrated by

Emily Arnold McCully

CLARION BOOKS • New York

For Sean, who loves cats
—T. W.

For Betsy
—E. A. M.

Clarion Books
a Houghton Mifflin Company imprint
215 Park Avenue South, New York, NY 10003
Text copyright © 2007 by Thérèse W. Gullickson
Illustrations copyright © 2007 by Emily Arnold McCully

The illustrations were executed in watercolor.
The text was set in Zipty Do.

www.clarionbooks.com

Printed in Malaysia

Library of Congress Cataloging-in-Publication Data
Weaver, Tess.
Cat jumped in! / by Tess Weaver ; illustrated by Emily Arnold McCully.
    p. cm.
Summary: An inquisitive feline walks through the rooms of a house, jumping into one mess
after another, before landing in the loving arms of its owner.
ISBN 978-0-618-61488-2
1. Cats—Juvenile fiction. [1. Cats—Fiction.] I. McCully, Emily Arnold, ill. II. Title.
PZ10.3.W355Cat 2007   [E]—dc22   2006039217

ISBN-13: 978-0-618-61488-2   ISBN-10: 0-618-61488-5

TWP 10 9 8 7 6 5 4 3 2 1

It was summer, and someone
left the window open.

Cat jumped in!

He sidled across a circle of pie dough,

licked a puddle of cream,

and sniffed something fishy . . .

somewhere in the kitchen.

WHAT was it?

WHERE was it?

Cat snooped around.

THERE!

Whoosh!

Cat dove in.

Down,

down,

down

he tumbled through
gooey eggshells
and syrupy waffles.

up

up,

Up,

he climbed over
apple cores and
banana peels.

Tip-tap,
      pitter-pat

   came footsteps, closer and closer.

"Cat?

Out!"

Oooooops!

Cat dashed away.

Someone left the closet door open.

Cat crept in.

He rubbed against heavy winter coats.
He climbed over boots and umbrellas.
He batted a scarf dangling from a hanger.

Then Cat spied a hat on the shelf.
A hat with feathers.

Cat jumped up.

CRRRAAAACKKK!

Down fell the shelf.

Down fell Cat.

Down fell the hat.

Someone left the bedroom door open.

Cat snuck in.

He sniffed pillows and blankets.

He stepped over fancy bottles.

He pounced on a powder puff.

Then Cat stopped and stared.

Who?

What?

Cat?

Cat couldn't believe his eyes!
A strange cat was staring at him.

Cat hissed,

"SSSS!"

The other cat hissed, too.

"SSSSS!"

Cat twitched his tail ᵘᵖ and down.

The stranger twitched his tail ᵘᵖ and down.

22

Cat inched closer . . . closer . . .

Then he poked the cat with
one paw and jumped back.

Thwump!

Down
fell
Cat.
Down
fell
bottles
and jewelry
and powder.

Plink!

Plink!

Plink!

Tip-tap, tip-tap, pitter-pat, pitter-pat!

"Cat? Out!"

OOOoooooOOOOppppppPPPPPSSSS!

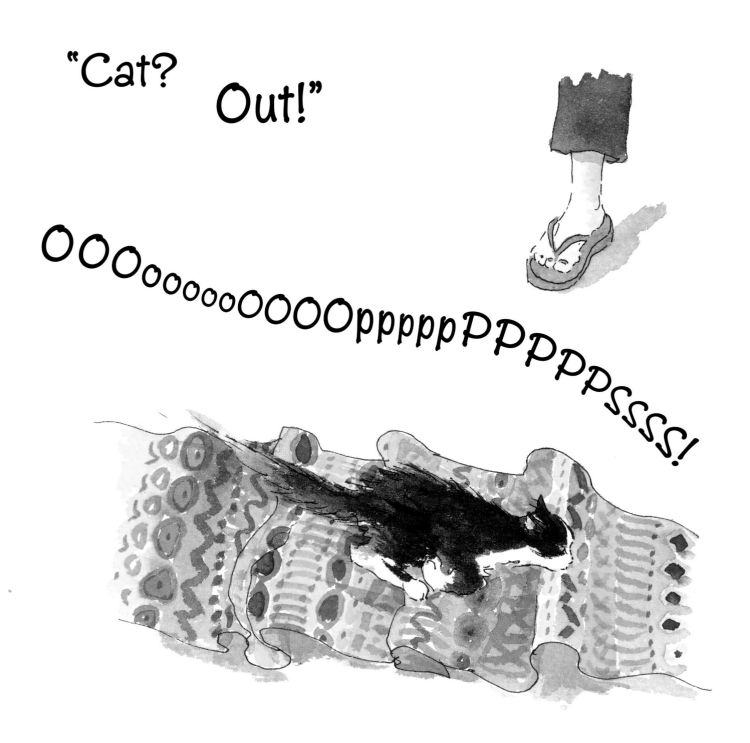

Cat rushed off.

Someone left the studio door open.

Cat slipped in.

He walked across something wet and sticky . . .
and stopped for a drink.

Then he lifted a front paw and shook it.

He lifted a back paw and shook it.

He shook his head and his tail,
his ears and his belly.

He wanted that paint
off, *off*, *OFF!*

The paint flew
on, *on*, *ON* . . .
nearly everywhere.

Tip-tap, tip-tap,
　　pitter-pitter-pat-PAT!

"Cat? Out!"

OOOOooppppPPPSSSSS!

Cat ran under a table.
He scooted back as far as he could go.

Someone sighed.
She drummed her fingers on the table.
Then she spied Cat's artwork in the middle
of the floor.

Someone looked at it for a very long time.

Slowly, Cat crept out from the shadows.
Cautiously, he curled his tail around
someone's ankles.

"Meow!"

"Here, Cat," someone answered softly.
She opened her arms and . . .

Cat jumped in!